Follow Those Feet!

by Christine Ricci
illustrated by Susan Hall

Ready-to-Read

Simon Spotlight/Nick Jr.

New York   London   Toronto   Sydney   Singapore

Based on the TV series *Dora the Explorer*® as seen on Nick Jr.®

SIMON SPOTLIGHT
An imprint of Simon & Schuster Children's Publishing Division
1230 Avenue of the Americas,
New York, New York 10020
Copyright © 2003 Viacom International Inc.
All rights reserved. NICKELODEON, NICK JR., *Dora the Explorer,*
and all related titles, logos, and characters are trademarks of Viacom International Inc.
All rights reserved, including the right of reproduction in whole or in part in any form.
READY-TO-READ, SIMON SPOTLIGHT, and colophon are
registered trademarks of Simon & Schuster.
Manufactured in the United States of America

12 14 16 18 20 19 17 15 13

Library of Congress Cataloging-in-Publication Data
Ricci, Christine.
Follow Those Feet! / by Christine Ricci.
p. cm.—(Ready-to-read ; 2)
Summary: Dora and Boots have found some strange footprints in the sandbox,
and need the reader's help to discover who—or what—made them.
Features rebuses.
ISBN 0-689-85239-8
1. Rebuses. [1. Animal tracks—Fiction. 2. Footprints—Fiction. 3. Rebuses.]
I. Title. II. Series.
PZ7.R355 Wh 2003
[E]—dc21
2002004826

Hi! I am 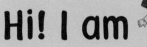. and I found

some in the .

I wonder who made them.

Do you know?

Did I make these ?

FOOTPRINTS

No, my feet are small.
I did not make these .

FOOTPRINTS

Did  make these ?
BOOTS FOOTPRINTS
No, his are shaped
FOOTPRINTS
like an oval. He did not
make these .
FOOTPRINTS

Who made these ?

FOOTPRINTS

We can follow them to find out.

Hello, 🐔 !
BIG RED CHICKEN

Did you make these 👣 ?
FOOTPRINTS

No, his feet have three toes! He did not make these .

FOOTPRINTS

Did the  make these ?

HORSE

FOOTPRINTS

No, the horse wears **HORSESHOES** on her feet. She did not make these **FOOTPRINTS**.

Did the  make these footprints?

No, the  has long

CROCODILE

nails. He did not make

these .

FOOTPRINTS

Did the  RABBIT make the FOOTPRINTS ?

No, she has two long feet and two short feet.

She did not make these

FOOTPRINTS

Did the 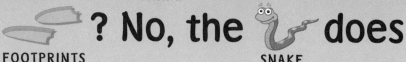 make these  ? No, the 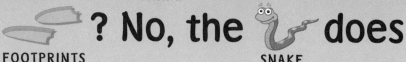 does not have feet!

SNAKE

FOOTPRINTS

SNAKE

He slides across the ground. He did not make these  .

FOOTPRINTS

Do you see 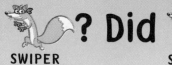? Did

SWIPER   SWIPER

make these ?

FOOTPRINTS

No,  is sneaky!
SWIPER

He tiptoes. He did not

make these .
FOOTPRINTS

The  go all the way to

FOOTPRINTS

the beach!

They go by the 🐚🐚
SHELLS

toward the 🏰 .
SAND CASTLE

Now do you know who
made these ?

FOOTPRINTS

It was ! He walked to
the beach in his new ⩗ !

BENNY

FLIPPERS

Yay! We did it! We found
out who made the !

FOOTPRINTS